Sound at Sight

guitar

by Lee Sollory

TRINITY · FABER

Faber Music Bloomsbury House 74–77 Great Russell Street London WC1B 3DA

in association with

Trinity College London 89 Albert Embankment London SE1 7TP

Sound at Sight

Sight reading requires you to be able to read and understand music notation, then convert sight into sound and perform a piece. This involves imagining the sound of the music before playing it, which in turn requires familiarity with intervals, chord shapes, rhythmic patterns and textures. The material in this series will help players to develop their skills and build confidence.

Examination sight reading

You have half a minute to prepare your performance. Use this time wisely:

- Check the key and time signatures. You might want to remind yourself of the scale and arpeggio, checking for signs of major or minor first.

- Look for any accidentals, particularly when they apply to more than one note in the bar.

- Set the pace in your head and read through the piece, imagining the sound. It might help to sing part of the music or to clap or tap the rhythm. You can also try out any part of the test if you want to.

- Have you imagined the effect of the dynamics?

When the examiner asks you to play the piece, do not forget the pace you have set. Fluency is more important than anything else: make sure that you keep going whatever happens. If you make a little slip, do not go back and change it. Give a performance of the piece: if you can play the pieces in this book you will be well prepared, so enjoy the opportunity to play another piece that you didn't know beforehand.

© 2004 by Faber Music Ltd and Trinity College London
First published in 2004 by Faber Music Ltd
in association with Trinity College London
Bloomsbury House 74–77 Great Russell Street London WC1B 3DA
Music processing by Robin Hagues
Printed in England by Caligraving Ltd
ISBN10: 0-571-52278-5
EAN13: 978-0-571-52278-1

To buy Faber Music or Trinity publications or to find out about the full range of titles available
please contact your local music retailer or Faber Music sales enquiries:

Faber Music Ltd, Burnt Mill, Elizabeth Way, Harlow CM20 2HX
Tel: +44 (0)1279 82 89 82   Fax: +44 (0)1279 82 89 83
sales@fabermusic.com   fabermusic.com   trinityguildhall.co.uk

• Initial   Fretted trebles and open basses only are used for this grade.

• Grade 1 Using notes within the first position and adding some variation to the dynamics.

• **Grade 2** Introducing ¾ time and simple ties, still within first position.

7

Allegretto

8

Moderato

9

Allegretto

10

Allegretto

11

Moderato

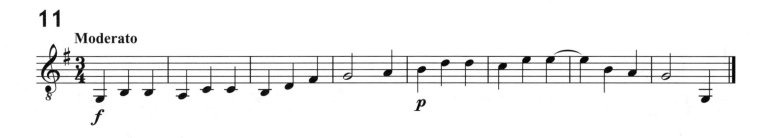

12

Moderato

• **Grade 3**   Including simple shifts and notes in the second position. Two-note chords and open bass are also introduced.

Sound at Sight

Also available:

Sound at Sight Guitar Grades 4-8
ISBN 0-571-52279-3

This book offers a wealth of approachable and attractive sight reading pieces which are carefully graded to match Trinity's requirements: invaluable practice material for guitarists and vital preparation for Trinity examinations Grades 4 to 8.